絲絲森林逗毛毛

Gill Davies 著

Eric Kincaid 繪

洪敦信 譯

三民書局

Haunted House   ISBN 1 85854 775 X

Written by Gill Davies and illustrated by Eric Kincaid

First published in 1998

Under the title Haunted House

by Brimax Books Limited

4/5 Studlands Park Ind. Estate,

Newmarket, Suffolk, CB8 7AU

毛毛美麗的尾巴

Fluffytuft's Wonderful Tail

Fluffytuft has a wonderful tail. It is **bushy** and red, and he is very proud of it. But he cannot see it easily. When Fluffytuft

twists around his tail always whisks out of **view**. Trying to look at it in the mirror, Fluffytuft **bounces** up and down on the bed. But still he can catch only a **glimpse** as his handsome tail **flashes** past.

毛毛有一條美極了的尾巴。它毛茸茸又紅通通的,所以他非常地引以為傲!可是他沒法兒輕易地見到它。當他扭轉身體時,他的尾巴總是從他的視線中掃過。毛毛在床上跳上跳下,想試著從鏡子裡看到它,可是他仍然只能在他那美麗的尾巴閃過去的時候,稍稍瞥見它一眼。

One lovely summer afternoon Fluffytuft goes to the Silver Pool at the **edge** of Silk Wood. "Now," he says, "I shall be able to see my tail **properly**. It will be **reflected** in the **shining** lake if I stand in the right place."

"Where is the best **spot** to get a good view of my tail?" Fluffytuft asks Glurk the Frog, who is sitting on a lily pad. Glurk **croaks** and sings his answer:

edge [ɛdʒ]
名 邊緣

properly [ˋprɑpɚlɪ]
副 恰好地，完全地

reflect [rɪˋflɛkt]
動 反射，映照

shining [ˋʃaɪnɪŋ]
形 閃爍的

spot [spɑt]
名 地點

croak [krok]
動 呱呱叫

一個美好的夏日午後，毛毛走到絲絲森林邊邊的銀池。
「現在，」他說，「我應該能完完全全地看到我的尾巴了吧！如果我站對了位置，尾巴應該會映照在閃亮的湖裡。」
「哪兒的位置最好，能看到我的尾巴呢？」毛毛問坐在蓮葉上的青蛙葛樂克。葛樂克呱呱地唱出他的回答：

"Over Buttercup Meadow,
Beyond the willow tree
Where the sun slants down
And the breeze flies free."

Glurk is right. The
water makes a
perfect mirror there.
Fluffytuft stares into the water and can see
a handsome, fluffy, red tail.
"Wow!" he says. "Is that wonderful tail really
mine?"
"Certainly not!" a voice answers, "It is mine!"

「越過金鳳花的草地，在那株柳樹的後頭，太陽在那兒斜下，微風自在地飛舞。」

葛樂克是對的。那裡的池水是一面最完美的鏡子。毛毛凝視著池水，果然看見一條毛茸茸的漂亮紅尾巴。

「哇！」他叫了起來。「那條美麗的尾巴真的是我的嗎？」

「當然不是囉！」一個聲音回應著，「它是我的！」

There, smiling at him, is a **cheeky**, little fox **cub** called Frisky. "That tail in the water is **definitely** mine," says Fluffytuft. "Since you seem so friendly, I do not like to **argue** the minute we meet," says Frisky. "But I **assure** you that tail is mine." Glurk says, "You are both wrong. Since you are standing close together, it looks like one tail. Move **apart**."

cheeky [ˈtʃikɪ]
形 無禮的

cub [kʌb]
名 幼獸

definitely [ˈdɛfənɪtlɪ]
副 絕對地

argue [ˈɑrgjʊ]
動 爭論

assure [əˈʃʊr]
動 向（人）保證

apart [əˈpɑrt]
副 分開地

站在那裡對著他微笑的，是一隻名叫福瑞斯基的無禮小狐狸。
「水裡的那條尾巴絕對是我的。」毛毛說。
「因為你看起來還蠻友善的，我不想在我們相遇的這一刻和你爭論。」福瑞斯基說。「但我向你保證，那條尾巴是我的。」
葛樂克說：「你們倆都錯了啦！因為你們倆站得太靠近了，所以看起來就好像一條尾巴。你們站開點兒。」

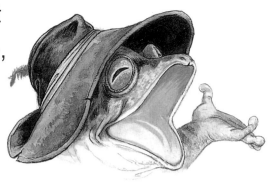

Frisky and Fluffytuft step apart; and there, reflected in the Silver Pool, are two **adorable**, fluffy, red tails.

The new friends play happily together all afternoon and **compare** their handsome, red tails as Glurk paints pictures of them.

Now Fluffytuft has a **portrait** to **hang** on the wall. He no longer needs to bounce up and down in front of the mirror to see his wonderful tail.

adorable [ə`dorəbl̩]
形 可愛的

compare [kəm`pɛr]
動 比較

portrait [`portret]
名 肖像畫

hang [hæŋ]
動 掛

福瑞斯基和毛毛便分開來站。映照在銀池裡的是兩條可愛的、毛茸茸的紅尾巴。整個下午，這對新朋友很愉快地玩在一起，還互相比較自己那美麗的紅尾巴，葛樂克則在一旁替他們倆畫了張畫。
現在毛毛有一幅可掛在牆上的肖像畫了。他再也不需要為了看他那條美麗的尾巴，在鏡子前面跳上跳下了。

驚喜的派對

The Surprise Party

Fluffytuft wakes up feeling **excited**. Today is Old Man Otter's birthday. The woodland **folk** are very fond of the lovely, kind, old otter and plan a **surprise** party that night.
Mrs Squirrel is baking a birthday cake. Mr Squirrel is making a new **deck chair** for Old Man Otter.
Fluffytuft says: "I want to make him a present too."

excited [ɪk`saɪtɪd]
形 興奮的

folk [fok]
名 一夥人

surprise [sə`praɪz]
名 驚喜

deck chair
躺椅

毛毛在興奮中起床，今天是水獺老曼的生日呢！森林裡的一夥動物都很喜歡這位可愛、心腸又好的老水獺，所以打算在今晚舉辦一個令他驚喜的派對。
松鼠媽媽在烤生日蛋糕。松鼠爸爸為水獺老曼做一張新的躺椅。
「我也想送他禮物。」毛毛說。

"**W**hy don't you lay him an egg?" says Mr Squirrel, laughing. Then Mrs Squirrel makes some **suggestions**.

"You could paint a nice picture."

"No," says Fluffytuft, "that is silly."

"Why not make a **calendar**?"

"That," says Fluffytuft, "is boring."

"What about a newspaper hat?"

"No," says Fluffytuft. "You have some really **stupid** ideas."

"Don't be rude!" says Mrs Squirrel, going into the **pantry** for flour.

---

suggestion
[səgˋdʒɛstʃən]
名 建議

calendar [ˋkæləndɚ]
名 月曆

stupid [ˋstjupɪd]
形 愚蠢的

pantry [ˋpæntrɪ]
名 儲物間

「你為什麼不為他下顆蛋呢？」松鼠爸爸笑著說，接著松鼠媽媽提出了一些建議。
「你可以畫一張漂亮的圖畫啊！」
「不要啦！」毛毛回答說，「那很蠢吔！」
「為什麼不做個月曆呢？」
「那個呀！」毛毛又說，「太無聊了！」
「那用報紙做頂帽子怎麼樣？」
「不要，」毛毛說。「妳的主意都太蠢了！」
「注意禮貌喔！」松鼠媽媽邊走進儲物間找麵粉邊說。

eeling cross, Fluffytuft goes out for a walk. He meets Rosie Rabbit. "What are you giving Old Man Otter for his birthday?" he asks.

"I don't know," says Rosie.

"Neither do I," says Fluffytuft, glad that he is not the only one who doesn't know. The two friends sit down to think, but they still have no ideas. Suddenly Frisky comes running along the path.

毛毛覺得不太高興，於是來到外頭散步。他遇到了兔子蘿西。

「妳打算送水獺老曼什麼生日禮物啊？」他問。

「我不知道耶！」蘿西回答。

「我也不知道耶！」毛毛說。他很高興不是只有他一個人不知道。他們兩個就坐下來想了想，可是仍然沒主意。這時，福瑞斯基突然沿著小徑跑了過來。

"Glurk the Frog has written a song about Old Man Otter," says Frisky. "He wants us to sing it at the birthday party tonight."

Frisky, Rosie and Fluffytuft practice the song all day. At last it is night.

Swans **glide** over the Silver Pool with **streamers** and balloons, and woodland folk carry **lanterns** as they gather around the lake's edge. Old Man Otter wakes up. He is **amazed** to see so many friends **clapping** and cheering for him.

glide [glaɪd]
動 滑行

streamer [`strimɚ]
名 彩帶

lantern [`læntɚn]
名 燈籠

amazed [ə`mezd]
形 驚訝的

clap [klæp]
動 拍手，鼓掌

「青蛙葛樂克寫了一首關於水獺老曼的歌呢！」福瑞斯基說。「他要我們在今晚的生日派對上演唱。」
福瑞斯基、蘿西和毛毛一整天都在練習那首歌。夜晚終於來臨了。
天鵝們帶著彩帶和氣球滑過銀池而來，森林裡的一夥動物也提著燈籠，聚集在湖邊。水獺老曼醒了。他很驚訝地看到這麼多朋友為他鼓掌、歡呼。

Old Man Otter is **thrilled** with his presents and birthday cake, but he loves the song best of all.
Glurk plays his **violin** as Fluffytuft, Rosie and Frisky sing sweetly;
"We love you so much, and we all agree, you're the dearest old man in the world, you see."
"This is the loveliest present of all," says Old Man Otter, tears running down his **whiskered** nose.
Then they all dance until **dawn**.

thrill [θrɪl]
⑩ 使激動

violin [ˌvaɪə`lɪn]
⑧ 小提琴

agree [ə`gri]
⑩ 同意

whiskered [`hwɪskəˑd]
⑱ 留鬍子的

dawn [dɔn]
⑧ 黎明

水獺老曼被禮物和生日蛋糕感動了，不過他最喜歡的是那首歌。葛樂克拉著小提琴，毛毛、蘿西和福瑞斯基甜美地唱著：「我們是多麼地愛你呀！我們一致同意，你是世界上最親愛的老水獺，你可知道？」
「這是所有禮物當中最棒的了。」水獺老曼說，眼淚沿著他那長滿鬍鬚的鼻子滴落下來。
大夥兒狂歡到黎明呢！。

兒童文學叢書

小 詩

有一種，在不遠不近的
林子裡邊，說：
「七就七，九歸九？」
（早安，吃飽了沒？）
我知道，牠們就是白頭翁。

（摘自《家是我放心的地方》
林煥彰／詩，施政廷／畫）

系列

在六點五點之間，
早起的鳥兒，
有很多種，不同的叫聲；

看故事學英文
我愛阿瑟系列

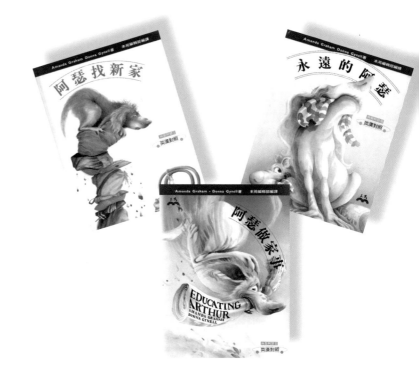

I LOVE ARTHUR

Amanda Graham・Donna Gynell著　本局編輯部編譯

20×27cm／精裝／3冊／30頁

阿瑟是一隻不起眼的小黃狗，為了討主人歡心，他什麼都願意做，但是，天啊！為什麼他就是一天到晚惹麻煩呢！？

一連三集，酷狗阿瑟搏命演出，要你笑得滿地找牙！

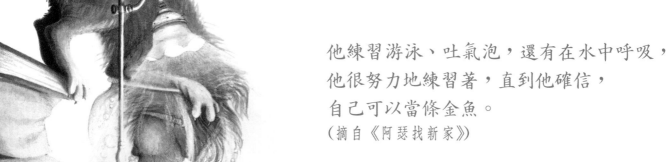

他練習游泳、吐氣泡，還有在水中呼吸，
他很努力地練習著，直到他確信，
自己可以當條金魚。
（摘自《阿瑟找新家》）

網際網路位址 http : // www. sanmin. com. tw

ⓒ 毛毛美麗的尾巴／驚喜的派對

著作人　Gill Davies
繪圖者　Eric Kincaid
譯　者　洪敦信
發行人　劉振強
著作財　三民書局股份有限公司
產權人
　　　　臺北市復興北路三八六號
發行所　三民書局股份有限公司
　　　　地址／臺北市復興北路三八六號
　　　　電話／二五〇〇六六〇〇
　　　　郵撥／〇〇〇九九九八——五號
印刷所　三民書局股份有限公司
門市部　復北店／臺北市復興北路三八六號
　　　　重南店／臺北市重慶南路一段六十一號
初　版　中華民國八十八年十一月
編　號　S85519

定　價　新臺幣壹佰捌拾元整

行政院新聞局登記證局版臺業字第〇二〇〇號

有著作權　不准侵害

ISBN　957-14-3073-0　（精裝）